GREG AND THE MURAL

BY **THALIA WIGGINS**
ILLUSTRATED BY **DON TATE**

magic wagon

Printed in the United States of America, Melrose Park, Illinois.
102011
012012

 This book contains at least 10% recycled materials.

Text by Thalia Wiggins
Illustrations by Don Tate
Edited by Stephanie Hedlund and Rochelle Baltzer
Cover and interior design by Neil Klinepier

Library of Congress Cataloging-in-Publication Data
Wiggins, Thalia, 1983-
  Greg and the mural / by Thalia Wiggins ; illustrated by Don Tate.
      p. cm. -- (Making choices. The McNair cousins)
  Summary: When Greg's design wins the contest for the mural in the new community center, he has to deal with the malicious anger of one of the losers, as well as the jealousy of his older cousin James.
  ISBN 978-1-61641-631-7
  1. Mural painting and decoration--Juvenile fiction. 2. Artists--Juvenile fiction. 3. Cousins--Juvenile fiction. 4. Jealousy--Juvenile fiction. 5. Vandalism--Juvenile fiction. 6. Trinidad--Juvenile fiction. [1. Mural painting and decoration--Fiction. 2. Cousins--Fiction. 3. Jealousy--Fiction. 4. Vandalism--Fiction.] I. Tate, Don, ill. II. Title.
  PZ7.W63856Gs 2012
  813.6--dc23
                                              2011027706

Contents

Good News for the Good Guy

Greg stifled a yawn as April pulled the van along the curb of his school. She accidentally let a tire graze the curb. The van ground to a halt.

"I'm gonna die!" Charles screamed, pretending to be scared. James and Greg laughed. April rolled her eyes.

"Quiet, Charles." Grandpa turned back to April. "Not bad, April. Just a little practice on pulling over to the side easily."

"Thanks, April!" Greg called as he jumped out of the van.

"Greg, over here!" It was Alex, Greg's best friend.

"*Hola*, Alex." Greg greeted Alex in Spanish.

"*Hola*." The boys bumped fists. They headed to the sixth grade classroom.

"So did the letter from the committee come yet?" Alex asked.

"No, not yet," Greg said. "Ms. Robinson will probably ask me the same question this afternoon in art class."

Greg was right. Ms. Robinson came to his table later that afternoon. The other students were busy working on their assignments.

"Greg, have you heard anything from the committee?" She lowered her voice so only he and Alex could hear.

"Nothing yet," Greg answered. He handed Alex some clay that they had to mold into miniature horses.

"I'm sure you won, Greg." She beamed at him. "You are a talented, hardworking young man. You deserve to win the mural contest."

"Thank you!" Greg said breathlessly. "I just wish the wait were over!"

Ms. Robinson patted him on the shoulder. "No worries. It's probably in today's mail." She walked away to help other students.

Later that day, Greg rushed home to see if the letter had arrived. He ran up the stairs to the mailbox and threw open the door. Nothing. Frowning, he went inside.

Greg was about to head upstairs to his room when his grandmother called out, "Greg, a letter just came for you. It's on the kitchen table."

Greg raced into the kitchen and scooped up the letter. His hands trembled as he tore open the envelope.

"Dear Gregory McNair," the letter began, "we apologize for the delay in declaring the winners of the 'My Dreams of Tomorrow Today!' mural contest. Your submission and another's tied for first place, which resulted in an extended week of deliberation.

"On behalf of the committee, we congratulate you on winning the grand prize of a scholarship to the college or private high school of your choice and your painting placed on the wall of the new community center in your neighborhood."

"Yes! I won!" Greg jumped in the air. He ran upstairs to tell his grandma.

"Grandma, I won!" Greg held the letter out to her. "I won!"

Grandma took the letter and pulled Greg in for a hug. "I knew you could do it! Sorry I won't be here to tell the others when they get home." She sat on her bed and read the letter. Greg joined her.

"Oh! There is a ceremony in two weeks," Grandma said. "There's going to be a kickoff and a ribbon-cutting ceremony right in front of the wall. Since the wall is located in front of the park, they are going to plant trees and flowers on a path leading up to the mural and the back entrance to the community center. The mayor is going to be there." She grinned at Greg. "Your picture will be in the paper!"

Grandma squeezed Greg's arm gently. "Luckily, both Grandpa and I are off that weekend. We can help out with the activities."

Greg smiled nervously and said, "It's all so overwhelming! I'm going to meet the mayor and have my picture taken! What if I have to give a speech?"

"If I know our mayor, he'll do the talking for you," Grandma said. She handed Greg the letter and got up. She smoothed her hotel uniform and headed for the stairs. Greg followed.

Just then, April, James, Charles, and Grandpa came home.

"Hey, Greg," Charles puffed, as he practiced using his crutches. "Did your letter come today?"

"Yeah!" Greg held it up for everyone to see. "I won!"

Everyone cheered. Grandma looked at her watch and sighed. "I've got to go to work. Why don't you all have pizza tonight? Love you all!"

Volunteers

Two weeks later, Greg couldn't help but smile as he walked out to the garden behind the community center. It seemed like everyone he knew came to celebrate his mural.

Greg's best friend, Alex, was there with his mother and his beautiful younger sister, Marina. She saw Greg looking at her and waved.

Greg blushed and quickly caught up with his family. They were heading to the front seats. He noticed his principal talking to Ms. Robinson.

"Look, it's the mayor," Charles pointed out to the rest of the family.

Greg took in the beautiful scene. The weather was comfortable. No clouds were in the sky.

"*Hola*, Greg." It was Alex, followed by his mother and Marina. Greg's stomach did more somersaults.

"*Hola*, Alex." Greg beamed. Then he turned to Alex's mother and sister. He broke out in a sweat.

"*Hola*, Senora Ramirez. *H-Hola*, Marina," Greg stammered.

"*Hola,*" Marina said with a smile. "Congratulations on your mural. That is totally cool."

"Thanks." Greg felt the heat rise on his neck.

Alex spoke up. "Ms. Robinson suggested he enter the mural contest. Greg didn't hesitate."

Alex put an arm around Greg. "Greg asked me and a few other kids what we would like to be when we grow up, and he decided to sketch and paint us as adults working in our careers," Alex told his mom.

"I want to be a businessman," Alex continued, "so Greg drew me as a man in a suit talking in front of a group of people. James wants to play basketball, so he drew him doing a slam dunk. Greg even drew himself as a graphic designer. Isn't that right, Greg?"

Greg blushed and stared straight at the ground. "Yeah."

"There's his picture. Right over there." Alex pointed at Greg's painting placed on a table a few feet away from the mayor. The table stood beside a wall where the mural was to be painted. A line of ribbon was in front of the wall. Alex led his sister over to the painting.

Greg sighed and slumped in his chair. Then, a voice behind him made him jump.

"Man, you really need to learn how to talk to girls." James laughed.

Greg's cheeks burned. He was embarrassed that James had noticed how nervous Greg was around Marina. Afterall, he was only eleven!

Right then, the mayor walked on stage and held his hand up for silence.

"I want to thank an outstanding young man for his hard work. Not only did he work hard for his painting to be placed on this wall, but he is an honor roll student. And, he helps his neighbors. It is a pleasure to present him with this scholarship. I am pleased to announce the mural winner, Greg McNair—or as his friends and family call him, Greg the Good."

A round of applause filled the air. Greg blushed as he walked up to the mayor. He waved to his friends and family from the stage. Then, he posed with the mayor and was almost blinded by the flashing of the cameras.

The mayor led Greg to the wall where his mural would be painted. He handed Greg a pair of oversize scissors to cut the ribbon.

"Ready, Greg?" The mayor smiled.

"Ready!" Greg said.

Together, they cut the red ribbon. The crowd cheered when pieces of red silk floated to the ground. Greg picked up a piece of ribbon and held it up.

Then, everybody got to work. Volunteers began painting the mural. More volunteers planted trees and flowers, did face painting, and handed out snacks.

James and Greg painted along with their friends.

"Wow!" James's friend Moochie rotated his shoulder. "My arm is still sore from basketball practice."

"I never knew that painting could be such hard work." Troy scowled.

"You two are acting like girls," James said.

"Excuse me!" Marina said, putting her hands on her hips.

"I mean . . ." James rolled his eyes. "You two need to toughen up!"

Moochie and Troy continued working, mumbling under their breath.

"So, Greg, when will the mural be done?" Marina picked up a spare paintbrush and began to paint next to Greg.

Greg cleared his throat. He started to sweat. "We have volunteers to help out every day after school. Ms. Robinson predicts that with a steady flow of volunteers, we should be done in three months. But the new garden will be done in a couple of weeks."

"Great!" Alex joined them. "Count me in to help when I don't have karate."

Marina sighed. "I want to help, but I have band practice and I entered the Mathathon Marathon."

Greg turned to her, interested. "Is that the citywide math contest between elementary schools?"

Marina nodded. "I love math. I want to be an engineer when I grow up."

"Cool," Greg said.

James and his friends made kissing sounds.

"Grow up!" Marina exclaimed. Then, she went back to painting.

"I was wrong, Greg!" James punched Greg playfully on the arm. "Some girls do like the good guys."

Everybody except Greg laughed.

The Crush 'Em Boys

"Thanks, Greg. I know that must have hurt your shoulders," Charles said when Greg helped him with his wheelchair. Greg and his family were walking home from the center a week after the ribbon-cutting ceremony.

"No problem." Greg groaned a little. "We've been painting for over a week, and I'm getting used to having sore muscles."

"It's too bad Grandpa had to work late," April said. "I could have borrowed the van to take us home."

"No thanks, April, I'm not in the mood to die anytime soon," Charles said. "You drive too fast for me!"

"Be quiet, you little bug!" April put her hand in his face.

As they passed the convenience store, they noticed fresh graffiti on the wall.

"Crush 'Em Boys?" James sucked his teeth. "Who are those clowns?"

"Some wannabe tough boys our age who live on top of the hill," Moochie said.

"They're crazy if they think they can just come in our neighborhood and start tagging walls!" Troy declared.

"Yeah they should know better than to mess with us!" James held up his arms and flexed his muscles.

"Yeah! We're Rock's Boys. We'll crush and mush them Crush 'Em Boys!" Moochie said.

"So what are you going to do?" Greg asked, half-jokingly. "Go in their neighborhood and tag their walls?"

"Hey, we do what we have to do to let them know we're not scared of them!" James exclaimed.

"Yeah," Moochie said. "We do what we have to do!" He turned to James. "What *are* we going to do, though?"

Greg, April, and Charles looked at each other and rolled their eyes.

Tagging

A few weeks later, Alex and Greg were working on the mural again. After an hour, Alex looked at his watch. "I have to go catch my bus."

"I'll walk with you." Greg gathered his belongings.

They said good-bye to Ms. Robinson and the other volunteers.

"If we keep walking this way, we'll be heading up the hill to the Crush 'Em Boys territory." Greg pointed to a hill a few miles away. The rooftops of the apartment buildings glistened in the setting sun.

"Yeah, I saw some graffiti on the bus over here and on a couple of buildings." Alex shook his head in disgust. "Some of the graffiti said stuff about your cousin."

"There's a fresh one!" Greg cried as they walked. The boys looked at another Crush 'Em Boys graffiti tag on a wall of an apartment building.

"I wish people knew that graffiti is annoying," Alex said. He turned to Greg. "Now, your mural—that's art!"

"Thanks." Greg smiled briefly. "Did you know that James swore he was going to look for the boys who are doing this?"

Alex gasped. "He better not. He'd get hurt."

The boys crossed the street to get to the bus stop when a bike flew by them.

Alex exclaimed, "Watch where you're going!"

The boy stopped his bike and turned. "What did you say to me?" He jumped off his bike and stomped toward Alex and Greg.

Alex tensed as the boy drew nearer. He was a foot taller than Alex and Greg.

"You're Greg the Good, huh?" the boy asked. He eyed Greg.

"Y-yes?" Greg's eyes widened.

"My name's Mark." He got within inches of Greg's face. "I entered that mural contest that you won. It should have been me!" Mark poked his finger in Greg's chest. "I'm the better artist!"

"Well, the judges didn't think so!" Alex managed to step in between the two boys. "So the best man won!"

Just then, James and his friends appeared on their bikes. They were heading home from the recreation center.

"What's going on?" James shouted. He got off his bike and into Mark's face. "Who are you?"

"I'm Mark—as in I always hit my mark!" he raised his fists up to show what he meant.

"Oh, really?" James burst out laughing.

"He doesn't know who he's messing with, right, Rock?" Troy said.

Mark smiled wickedly at James. "So you're Rock, eh? We at the top of the hill have been waiting to meet you!"

Greg saw James's face change from surprise to deep hate. "You're a Crush 'Em Boy?"

"That's right!" Mark pushed James. "So you better watch out or—"

James had Mark on the ground before Greg could yell, "No!"

"Looks like the Crush 'Em Boy got crushed!" James laughed. His friends joined in the laughter.

Mark sprung up and grabbed his bike. "I'm going to get you, Rock!"

Greg watched Mark pedal away. "I think you just started something with the Crush 'Em Boys, don't you?"

James looked a little worried, then smiled. "Whatever those chumps have, we'll be ready for them! Right, guys?" James walked over to his friends.

I have a bad feeling about this, Greg thought.

James's Plan

"Man, I can't believe you're gonna be on the news again!" Charles exclaimed between bites of pizza. Greg was watching TV in the living room with his family.

"Yeah," April agreed. "How was it being interviewed this time?" She handed Greg a can of soda.

"It was okay. They just wanted an update on the mural." Greg took the soda. "The reporter met me in my art class. She spoke with Ms. Robinson. Ms. Robinson said I had earned my place as a top student."

"What time is it going to air?" Grandma Rose came into the room with a bowl of popcorn in one hand and a platter of carrot and celery sticks in the other.

"In a few minutes," Grandpa said and looked at his watch.

"Celery sticks? Oh, come on, Grandma! We're celebrating," Charles teased.

"You can still eat healthy while you're celebrating." Grandma scooped up a few sticks and placed them on his plate.

"Where's James?" Grandma asked. Everybody shrugged.

"He's probably upstairs," April said.

"I'll get him," Greg said. He raced up the stairs.

James's door was open just a crack. Greg was about to knock when he heard James talking.

"Moochie! Don't be scared. When we're done with them, the Crush 'Em Boys won't know what hit them!" James said.

Greg was about to put his ear to the door when it swung open. He lost his balance and fell on his back. He looked up to see James smiling down on him.

"Moochie, let me call you back," James said. Then, he hung up the phone.

"Well, well." James leaned down to his cousin. "Hear anything good?" He grabbed Greg's shirt by the collar and pulled him up.

"What are you going to do, James?" Greg struggled to get free. "Go out to

their neighborhood and start trouble? That will just make things worse!"

"They need to know that they can't mess with us!" James let go of Greg.

"I'm not scared of Mark," Greg said. Then he thought about it. "Well, maybe I am a little."

"That's why we have to protect ourselves and let them know that we won't back down!"

Greg stared at his cousin. Then he shook his head. As he did, something caught his eye. He saw a can of spray paint poking out of James's backpack.

"Spray p—!" Greg started to say loudly, but James covered his mouth.

"Quiet!" James hissed.

"Can't breathe!" came Greg's muffled voice. James released him.

"I can't believe you!" Greg's jaw dropped. "You're going to get yourself in more trouble."

"You wouldn't understand." James ushered Greg out into the hallway. He closed his bedroom door behind them.

"Not a word to Grandpa or I'll spray *Greg loves Marina* all over your mural!" James muttered as they went downstairs.

Greg stopped midway to face James. "You wouldn't!"

James chuckled and nudged him to go downstairs. "Now that you're a celebrity, I guess the girls will come in by the thousands."

"It's on!" Charles announced as the boys entered the living room.

"Greg McNair," the TV reporter said to Greg, "you have done amazing things in your community. You are also artistic." She turned away from Greg and motioned to a wall. "Here we have a nearly-completed replica of Greg's painting that won the 'My Dreams of Tomorrow Today!' mural contest. Greg beat out twenty-five other contestants here in the city . . ."

Everyone in the McNair household cheered for Greg. James offered a toast and they clinked soda cans.

Greg was grateful for that moment with his family. But in the back of his mind, he was worried about James and what was yet to come.

Good Cousin vs. Bad Cousin

When the bell rang at the end of the next day, Greg left his last classroom and saw Grandpa heading to the principal's office. Greg knew it wasn't good to see Grandpa at school.

"Hey, Grandpa." Greg looked at his worried face. "Is everything okay?"

"I just have to talk to your principal about your cousin." Grandpa tried to smile. "Go wait in the van."

Greg had known it would only be a matter of time before James got into trouble again.

He should have known better than to mess with those boys, Greg thought as he hopped in the van.

Charles was already in the backseat.

"Did you hear James spray painted some bad words about the Crush 'Em Boys on the convenience store? They got it on camera," Charles told Greg.

Greg groaned. "When will he learn?"

Shortly after, James came to the car, followed by Grandpa. Grandpa started the car.

"Why, James?" Grandpa asked without looking at him.

"I'm sorry, Grandpa. I was just trying to show those boys that we aren't afraid of them! They've been tagging our neighborhood, so we decided to tag theirs!"

"So you go around with those boys calling yourselves 'Rock's Boys' to prove you're big and bad and cause trouble?" Grandpa asked. "Then they come here and cause more trouble! The cycle continues and nothing good comes out of it. Someone could end up hurt or worse! To prove what?"

Grandpa waited until they had stopped at a red light before looking at

James. "I keep trying to do good by you, and you never seem to do right, James! Why can't you be more like Greg?"

James sank down in his seat and folded his arms.

At home, Grandma met them at the front door. She had on her hotel uniform.

"So what did the school say?" she asked Grandpa.

"He's suspended," Grandpa sighed. "And he has to clean up the graffiti. Officer Jackson will be here Saturday morning to pick him up. I don't know what I'm going to do with him."

Grandma hugged Grandpa. "We just keep trying, dear. The casserole is in the oven. It should be ready in an hour." She headed out the door.

As she passed, Greg noticed tears in her eyes. Greg felt ashamed that James was the one who made the family look bad.

James slowly made his way upstairs. Before Greg could think, he blurted out, "I wish we weren't cousins!"

James turned around. Greg saw the look of hurt, shock, and anger on James's face. "What did you say?"

"I said I wish I wasn't your cousin!" Greg said as he approached the steps. "You're always causing problems! I try hard to bring honor to this family, and you're always messing it up!"

"You're no better than I am, Greg! We are more alike than you think!" James jumped down the stairs and confronted Greg.

Greg stood his ground. He was so angry he couldn't help himself. "Even before the mural you were always the one causing trouble!" Greg hissed. "Why don't you just leave and never come back?"

"No!" Charles screamed.

Greg knew his cousin's fighting style well. James aimed his right fist for Greg. Greg ducked and then hit James squarely in the nose before James punched him in the eye.

"Stop it!" April grabbed James and struggled until Grandpa rushed in.

"What's going on?" Grandpa roared. He noticed April struggling with all her might to keep James off of Greg. He rushed to grab James. Blood flowed from James's nose.

Greg felt like his head would burst. He looked up at James and said, "I hate you!"

Without a word, James shrugged off Grandpa and marched out the door.

Greg stood up and burst into tears. Grandpa gave him a hug. "I'm sorry! He made Grandma cry and . . . and . . . I'm so sorry!"

Grandpa sighed. "I'm disappointed in you for letting your anger get the best of you." Grandpa sounded as if he were talking to himself.

"I just hope he doesn't go and do something stupid!" Charles said.

"Yeah," Grandpa said as he examined Greg's eye. "Let's get some ice on that."

Family Matters

Greg took the ice pack off his eye and glanced at the clock. James had been gone for two hours. Greg came downstairs to find Grandpa pacing in the living room.

Greg felt ashamed of himself. *Do I really think I'm better than James? Maybe I do,* Greg thought miserably as he headed for the kitchen. *It's hard not to when I get rewarded for the good I do and James gets punished for doing wrong. But it's his decision to keep doing bad things!*

Grandpa came into the kitchen minutes later carrying the phone. "I called Grandma and she said to let Officer Jackson know. I just called him and he said he will look for James." Grandpa sat in a chair.

"Grandma reminded me that James is family. We can't pick and choose who our family members are, but they are our family," Grandpa said. "We have to try to love them no matter what. I just hope that James can see the light before something bad happens."

"Me too." Greg put a fresh ice pack on his eye.

The phone rang seconds later. Grandpa scrambled to answer it.

"Y-yes?" he stammered. "Officer Jackson, you have him? Where?" Grandpa was silent on the phone for a minute.

"He was at the top of the hill." Grandpa was angry. "Okay. Bring him home."

Grandpa scowled as he hung up the phone. Greg just shook his head.

When Officer Jackson brought James home, Grandpa told him his punishment. James wasn't allowed to practice basketball.

For the next few weeks, James hardly acknowledged Greg. At home, James avoided the rest of the family and did not join them for dinner.

Greg felt bad about the fight with his cousin. He didn't want to admit it, but he missed James.

James makes me laugh, **Greg** thought. *Even though he causes trouble, James really tries his best to protect me from other*

neighborhood bullies. Of course that never stopped him from picking on me himself!

Greg was so deep in thought that he almost forgot he was at the unveiling ceremony of his mural.

"Let's pose for the camera once more, Greg." The mayor nudged Greg out of his daydream. Greg forced himself to smile in front of strangers, classmates, teachers, and his family.

Greg looked over at his family. James was missing. The argument he and James had before their fight kept replaying in his head.

I don't think I'm better than James, **Greg told himself** as the flashing camera lights blinded him. *I just choose to do different things to achieve my goals. Besides, what did he mean by 'We are more alike than you* *think'? I'm nothing like James! How could he say that?*

A huge curtain hung in front of the now-completed mural. The mayor handed Greg the rope that would lower the curtain to display the painting.

Out of the corner of his eye, Greg saw James making his way into the crowd. He was trying to scream something, but Greg couldn't hear him over the noise.

"What?" Greg started to walk over to him, but the mayor stopped him.

"We're on a tight schedule," He explained. "We need to hurry." He motioned for Greg to pull the rope.

What does James want to tell me? Greg wondered as he pulled the rope down.

There was a gasp and a hush from the crowd. Greg looked at the mural and

cried out. Someone had spray painted some very bad words about James and Greg on the mural.

Now Greg knew what James meant about how alike the two of them were. At that moment, Greg wanted nothing more than to crush the Crush 'Em Boys—starting with Mark!

The McNairs were all silent on the ride home. Greg waited until they were all inside the house before he broke down.

"Let me at them!" Greg screamed, tears staining his cheeks. He wanted revenge!

"Greg, calm down." Grandma Rose sat by his side. She didn't know what to do.

Then, James came out of the corner, sat on the other side, and put an arm around Greg. He allowed his cousin to cry on his shoulder.

"I'm sorry," James said, his voice cracking. "I found out too late. I didn't want you to see—" he sniffed. "I didn't mean for this to happen."

Cousins Team Up

Just then there was a light tap on the door. It was Officer Jackson. He looked at both Greg and James and asked, "Do either of you know anything that can help us find out who did this?"

"It was Mark!" Greg sneered. "I hope you find him before I do!"

"Greg!" Grandpa snapped. "Don't tell me you're thinking about going to find those boys?"

"Why not?" Greg demanded. "It's what James is going to do!" He turned to James. "Right?"

James straightened up and smiled. "Actually, I think we could use a little police help on this one."

Greg's jaw dropped. So did everyone else's in the room. James laughed at everyone's expressions. "I've got a plan!"

The next day Greg, James, and their friends made their way up the hill on their bikes.

As Greg pedaled up the hill, he took in the dirty-looking apartment buildings. Some of them had broken windows, but people still lived in them.

"Wow," Greg said. "I didn't know people lived like this."

"Welcome to the real world," Troy said. "My cousin stays up here."

As they continued, Greg counted at least seven different Crush 'Em Boys tags on walls of shops and in alleys.

"Don't they care about how messy their neighborhood looks?" Greg said.

"It kind of looks like ours," Moochie said ashamedly. "I didn't think that tagging their buildings would end up this badly."

The boys were near the top of the hill when they heard thunder.

"M-maybe we should turn back," Moochie stammered. "I don't like thunder!"

"Don't be a punk!" James barked. He continued on. They went up a couple more blocks before James stopped.

They all stopped beside him. He pointed to an alley behind an old gas station. Silently, they watched a group of boys duck behind the building. Greg could tell instantly that Mark was one of the boys. He shuddered.

"Let's do this!" James pedaled slowly over. The boys cautiously followed.

James used hand signals to tell them when to stop, speed up, and slow down. When they reached the corner of the building, James signaled for them to stop.

"You stay here," he whispered to Greg.

"What?" Greg said. "No way! I'm going!"

"I'll stay!" Moochie interjected.

"Shh! Grandpa would kill me if anything happened to you. Besides, I'm the bad boy, right?" He winked at Greg. "This is what I do."

Greg couldn't help but smile back. He nodded and let James and his friends pass.

Soon it began to rain. Greg pulled his hood over his head and looked up and down the street. He didn't see one police car.

Where are the police? Greg wondered. *What's taking them so long?* Suddenly, Greg heard sounds coming from the alley.

"James!" Greg was about to pedal to his cousin when he heard bikes coming his way.

"Greg! Get out of here!" It was Moochie. He almost hit Greg when his bike swerved on the wet pavement.

"Wait! Where's James?" Greg called. But Moochie was gone.

Lightning quickly lit the darkened sky. Three more boys on bikes zoomed by Greg. He couldn't tell if they were friends or Crush 'Em Boys. Greg made a quick decision. He had to find James.

Greg started to pedal after his cousin. He ignored the rain drenching him. He pedaled slowly down the alley. Suddenly he heard footsteps. He panicked and tried to turn back the way he came, but his bike slipped and he fell. The next thing he knew, he was on the ground and four boys were on him.

"We caught one!" a low voice barked.

"I w-was looking for my cousin," Greg stuttered, managing to sound innocent.

"Greg the Goofy, is that you?" said another. Greg groaned when he realized it was Mark.

Someone grabbed Greg by the shoulders to pick him up. Greg was face-to-face with Mark. Mark smiled when he looked into Greg's terrified eyes.

Greg was expecting Mark to punch him. But just then he heard another voice in the distance.

"Hey! Leave him alone!" It was James.

Greg gasped and turned to see his cousin and five other boys run toward him from the alley opening. The boy holding him dropped him and ran with the rest of his group. They ran to the other side of the alley only to have a police car pull up as they reached the street.

When James reached Greg, he slowed down. His friends went to chase the others into the hands of the cops.

"Are you okay?" James grabbed Greg by the shoulders and looked him over.

"Yeah, I'm fine." Greg rubbed his back.

Without warning, James hit him.

"Ouch!" Greg yelped. "What was that for?"

"For going in the alley to look for me! You were supposed to follow Moochie!"

"I was looking for you!" Greg squealed. "If anything happened to you—"

"Aw!" James put Greg in a headlock. "You're getting soft on me!"

"Watch the head!" Greg squirmed free.

James and Greg walked toward the police car. Moochie and the others were there watching the police arrest the boys.

"I didn't do anything!" Mark said to Officer Jackson.

"Really?" Officer Jackson motioned to another officer. "It appears we have your backpack, Mr. Mark Thomas. There are cans of spray paint that match the color of the new tag on the wall behind this store."

"Yeah! We got y'all!" Moochie bragged. "Now you have to do graffiti cleanup!"

"See you there!" Mark said as he was placed in a police car. "I'll make sure I stand right beside you, Moochie!"

Officer Jackson came over to James, Greg, and their friends. "Boys, this is Lieutenant Tracy. She and her team have been trying to catch those boys for some time."

"Good work, boys!" She shook hands with each of them. "I'm sure you all now know how bad graffiti makes our neighborhoods look. Defacing property can lead to a lot of trouble. Thank you for teaming up with us. You should be proud of the work you have done for your community."

James laughed. "It was fun hunting down the bad guys! Almost makes me want to be a cop."

They all stopped to stare at him. Officer Jackson's jaw dropped.

"What?" James winked. "A guy can't have a change of heart?"

Making Choices
Greg the Good

Every decision a person makes has a consequence. Greg made some decisions that earned him the nickname Greg the Good. Let's take a look:

Decision: Greg chose to enter a contest to better his community.

Consequence: Greg won and was rewarded with a scholarship and his work on display.

Decision: Greg chose not to get revenge by tagging neighborhoods with graffiti.

Consequence: Greg was part of the group that helped catch the taggers!

Making Choices
James the Rock

Every decision has a consequence. James made some decisions that got him in trouble. Let's take a look:

Decision: James chose to get back at the Crush 'Em Boys by tagging their neighborhood.
Consequence: Officer Jackson caught James tagging. James was suspended from school and forced to help clean up the graffiti.

Decision: James decided to work with police to solve a problem instead of taking matters into his own hands.
Consequence: The neighborhood bullies were caught and punished. And James found a new way to handle problems!

About the Author

Thalia Wiggins is a first-time author of children's books. She lives in Washington DC and enjoys imagining all of the choices Greg and James can make.

About the Illustrator

Don Tate is an award-winning illustrator and author of more than 40 books for children, including *Black All Around!*; *She Loved Baseball: The Effa Manley Story*; *It Jes' Happened: When Bill Traylor Started to Draw*; and *Duke Ellington's Nutcracker Suite*. Don lives in the Live Music Capitol of the World, Austin, Texas, with his wife and son.